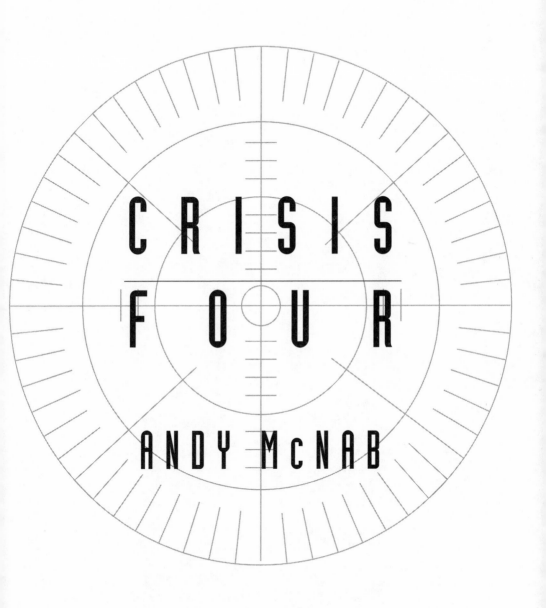

CRISIS FOUR

ANDY McNAB

BALLANTINE BOOKS

NEW YORK

A Ballantine Book
The Ballantine Publishing Group

Copyright © 1999 by Andy McNab

www.randomhouse.com/BB/

Library of Congress Card Number: 00-190285

ISBN 0-345-42807-2

Manufactured in the United States of America
First American Edition: July 2000
10 9 8 7 6 5 4 3 2 1